My dearest puppy, Storm,

hope this letter reaches you safe and
ound. You have been so brave since you had
 flee from the evil wolf Shadow.

o not worry about me. I will hide here
ntil you are strong enough to return and
ad our pack. For now you must move on –
ou must hide from Shadow and his spies.
 Shadow finds this letter I believe he will
 y to destroy it . . .

nd a good friend – someone to help finish
y message to you. Because what I have to
 y to you is important. What I have to say
 this: you must always

lease don't feel lonely. Trust in your friends
nd all will be well.

ur loving mother,

Canista

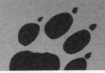

Sue Bentley's books for children often include animals, fairies and wildlife. She lives in Northampton and enjoys reading, going to the cinema, relaxing by her garden pond and watching the birds feeding their babies on the lawn. At school she was always getting told off for daydreaming or staring out of the window – but she now realizes that she was storing up ideas for when she became a writer. She has met and owned many cats and dogs and each one has brought a special kind of magic to her life.

Sue Bentley

Party Dreams

Illustrated by Angela Swan

PUFFIN

Published by the Penguin Group
Penguin Books Ltd, 80 Strand, London WC2R ORL, England
Penguin Group (USA) Inc., 375 Hudson Street, New York, New York 10014, USA
Penguin Group (Canada), 90 Eglinton Avenue East, Suite 700, Toronto, Ontario, Canada M4P 2Y3
(a division of Pearson Penguin Canada Inc.)
Penguin Ireland, 25 St Stephen's Green, Dublin 2, Ireland (a division of Penguin Books Ltd)
Penguin Group (Australia), 250 Camberwell Road, Camberwell, Victoria 3124, Australia
(a division of Pearson Australia Group Pty Ltd)
Penguin Books India Pvt Ltd, 11 Community Centre, Panchsheel Park, New Delhi – 110 017, India
Penguin Group (NZ), 67 Apollo Drive, Rosedale, North Shore 0632, New Zealand
(a division of Pearson New Zealand Ltd)
Penguin Books (South Africa) (Pty) Ltd, 24 Sturdee Avenue, Rosebank,
Johannesburg 2196, South Africa

Penguin Books Ltd, Registered Offices: 80 Strand, London WC2R ORL, England

puffinbooks.com

First published 2008
5

Text copyright © Sue Bentley, 2008
Illustrations copyright © Angela Swan, 2008
All rights reserved

The moral right of the author and illustrator has been asserted

Set in Bembo
Typeset by Palimpsest Book Production Limited,
Grangemouth, Stirlingshire
Made and printed in England by Clays Ltd, St Ives plc

British Library Cataloguing in Publication Data
A CIP catalogue record for this book is available from the British Library

ISBN: 978-0-141-32379-4

www.greenpenguin.co.uk

Penguin Books is committed to a sustainable future
for our business, our readers and our planet.
The book in your hands is made from paper
certified by the Forest Stewardship Council.

Prologue

The young silver-grey wolf bounded towards the stream that ran through the snow-covered valley. Dipping his head, Storm lapped at the clear icy water. It felt good to be home again.

Suddenly, a terrifying howl rose in the still air.

'Shadow!' Storm gasped. The fierce lone wolf who had attacked Storm's pack and left his mother wounded was very close.

In an instant, there was a bright gold flash and the young silver-grey wolf disappeared. Where Storm had been standing there was now a tiny spotted Dalmatian puppy with a pink muzzle, a wet black nose and huge midnight-blue eyes.

Storm's puppy heart beat fast and he started to tremble as he hoped this disguise would protect him. He must find somewhere to hide – and quickly.

There was a clump of snow-covered bushes some way upstream. Storm ran towards them, almost tripping over his own paws as they skidded on the hard snow. He was just about to leap into the bushes, when he saw the dark

shape of an adult wolf crouching
beneath them.

Storm gasped. Shadow was waiting to
ambush him! It was too late to run.
This was the end.

The adult wolf lifted its head.

'Storm! In here, quickly!'

'Mother!' Storm sighed with relief as
he recognized the gentle face of the
she-wolf.

He scrambled into the bushes, his
body wriggling and his short thin tail
wagging a greeting. Canista rumbled
affectionately as she licked her disguised
cub's smooth spotted fur. 'It is good to
see you, my son,' she growled softly.
'But you cannot stay. Shadow wants to
lead the Moon-claw pack, but the
others will not follow him while you

live. It is too dangerous for you right now.'

Storm growled and his midnight-blue eyes sparked with anger and fear. 'Shadow killed my father and three litter brothers, but he will not lead our pack. I will face him and fight him!'

Canista nodded. 'One day you will, Storm. But you are still too small and I am weak from Shadow's poisoned bite and cannot help you. Use this disguise. Go back to the other world and return when you are stronger.' As she stopped speaking, her eyes clouded with pain.

Storm whined with sympathy. He huffed out a puppy breath filled with tiny gold sparks. They swirled around Canista's injured paw, before sinking into her fur and disappearing.

'Thank you. The pain is easing,'
Canista sighed gratefully.

Suddenly, a dark shadow fell across
the bush where Storm and his mother
were hiding. Iron-hard paws scrabbled
at the packed snow as the fierce wolf
came closer.

'Come out, Storm! Let us end this
now!' Shadow challenged.

'Go! Save yourself!' Canista urged.

Storm whimpered and his big blue
eyes widened as he felt the power
building inside his little body. Glittering
sparks ignited in his smooth spotted fur.
The golden light around him grew
brighter. And brighter . . .

Chapter
ONE

Paige Riley sat sulking in the back of
her step-dad's car. It wasn't fair. She'd
been right in the middle of talking
about birthday parties with her two
best friends, when Keith called to
collect her.

'Why couldn't Mum pick me up, like
we'd arranged? Then I could have
stayed another hour with Amy and Tori,'

Paige complained. 'Mum knows we always get excited because our birthdays all come so close together.'

'I'm sorry, love. I didn't want to say anything until we were by ourselves, but your mum's been taken into hospital,' Keith explained as he pulled away from the kerb. 'They've done tests and she and the baby are both fine, but she's going to have to stay in hospital and rest until he's born.'

Paige was glad it was nothing serious. 'Poor Mum. She hates hospitals. She won't like being stuck in there for weeks. It's a good thing half-term holidays start tomorrow. I'll be able to go and visit her every day and cheer her up.'

Keith glanced at her in the rear-view

mirror. 'Well, maybe not *every* day. I'm on nights for the next two weeks. So your mum and I think it's best if you stay with my mum for the time being.'

Paige wrinkled her nose. She'd never met Keith's mum, but she knew that she lived in a village out in the middle of nowhere. 'Do I have to? Can't I stay in town with Granny and Gramps Riley instead?' she asked.

'I'm afraid not. They're on holiday,'
Keith explained. 'I know Brookton
village is a bit remote, but I'll come
over and fetch you when I can and
take you to see your mum. By the
way, try not to call my mother Gran
or Nan, will you? She's a bit sensitive
about her age.'

'What shall I call her then?'

'Her name's Deborah. She likes
everyone to call her Debs,' Keith said.

Paige snorted. Debs! What sort of
name was that for a step-gran? 'Anyway,
I don't need to go and stay with
anyone else. I can look after myself in
our flat. I'm not a baby. I'll be ten in
two weeks.'

Keith smiled. 'I know. And you're a
very grown-up sensible young lady. But

I don't like the idea of you being left by yourself all day *and* all night. Besides, your mum will feel happier knowing that you'll be taken care of. We can't have anything worrying her at a time like this, can we?' he said reasonably.

There was no answer to that. Paige knew when she was beaten. 'But what about my things? I need my jeans and trainers and —'

'I've already packed a case for you,' Keith interrupted. 'I can get anything else you want later. All right?'

Paige nodded miserably, her shoulders drooping. It wasn't all right. It was all wrong! This new baby had somehow managed to spoil things for her before he was even born! She probably wouldn't even be able to have a birthday party.

Her heart sank as she thought of Amy and Tori, who would still be planning their parties and deciding what to wear. There was no point in her joining in now.

Keith drove through town and out on to a country road. After what seemed like hours, he turned down a dark twisty lane and stopped in front of a large detached red-brick house. There was a light on in the porch and just as Paige reached the front door it creaked open.

A woman with tied-back dark hair, a flowing velvet top and jeans swooped out in a cloud of perfume. 'Hello, you must be Paige. Come in, darling. I'm really looking forward to getting to know you.'

Paige smiled stiffly, wishing she could say the same. 'Thanks for letting me stay with you, Mrs Stokes,' she said politely.

'Oh, call me Debs – everyone does,' Debs said, beaming as she ushered Paige into the house.

Paige stared at the coloured floor tiles and stained-glass windows. Old-fashioned glass wall lamps cast a dim glow over the rich wallpaper and dark paintwork. The house was like something out of a creepy ghost story. Paige wouldn't have been surprised to see giant bats hanging upside down from the ceiling.

Keith took her case upstairs and then came into the kitchen where Debs was filling the kettle. 'I'll get straight off then. They're expecting me back at work. Will you be OK, Paige?' he asked.

Paige nodded uneasily. She wasn't OK really. She hated this gloomy house and she didn't know what to make of Debs but she wasn't about to say so in front of everyone.

'I hope you'll be happy staying with me in my funny old house, even though I know that you must be

longing to be at home with your gorgeous new baby brother,' Debs said, smiling warmly.

You couldn't be more wrong, Paige thought, but she wisely stayed silent.

After Keith left, having promised to phone the following day, Debs made hot chocolate. As they sat drinking it, Paige stifled a yawn.

'You look worn out. This is all a bit sudden, isn't it? Come on, I'll show you your bedroom. Bring your drink with you,' Debs said kindly.

Paige trudged upstairs behind Debs. Her bedroom had the same rich wallpaper, dark paintwork and heavy furniture as the rest of the house. Paige blinked at the enormous four-poster bed that stood against one wall.

'Impressive, isn't it? That bed's been
in the family for donkey's years. I was
born in it and so was Keith,' Debs said
cheerily.

Yuck! Too much information, Paige
thought. 'I'd like to go to sleep now,
please,' she said hurriedly.

'Of course you would, darling. It's
been a long day. Sweet dreams. I'll see

you in the morning.' Debs closed the
door behind her.

Paige quickly undressed and brushed
her teeth at the big old-fashioned basin
before climbing into the vast bed. She
lay there shivering. Moonlight poured
in through the curtains, casting shadows
and making the dark furniture into
lumpish shapes.

Her tummy felt all tight and
churning. A wave of loneliness washed
over her. She wished her mum didn't
have to stay in hospital. This was all her
baby brother's fault.

Suddenly, a dazzling flash of bright
light lit up the whole room and Paige
gasped as her sad thoughts disappeared
with the darkness. She rubbed her eyes
in disbelief – at the bottom of the bed

seemed to be sitting a tiny figure, glowing with thousands of diamond points of light.

'Aargh! A ghost!' Paige gave a strangled scream and dived under the covers.

Chapter
TWO

Paige lay under her bed covers trembling
like a leaf, but nothing leapt on top of
her and the room seemed strangely
silent. Maybe she had imagined the
whole thing. After all she was really tired
and not feeling like herself at all.

Very slowly, Paige lowered the covers
and peeped over the top of them. 'Oh!'
she gasped.

To her complete amazement a tiny cute puppy with black spots on a smooth white coat and the brightest midnight-blue eyes she had ever seen was sitting on the bed.

Was it a ghost dog? Whatever it was, it wasn't glowing any more. In fact, it was blinking at her and wagging its slim spotty tail. Paige found herself smiling as her heartbeat began to return to

normal. She sat up properly and leaned back against the pillows.

'Hello! Aren't you gorgeous? I didn't know that Debs had a Dalmatian puppy!' She rubbed her fingers together encouragingly, hoping that the puppy wanted to make friends.

To her delight, it padded up the bed towards her and she felt its slight weight as it climbed on to her legs.

'I am sorry if I startled you,' the puppy woofed.

Paige did a double take and snatched back her hand. Maybe it was a ghost puppy after all! 'How come y-you can s-speak?' she stammered.

'Where I come from, all of my pack can speak,' the puppy yapped. Despite being so tiny it didn't seem to be too

afraid of her. 'I am Storm of the
Moon-claw pack. Who are you?'

Paige still couldn't believe this was
really happening, but her curiosity was
getting the better of her fear. She
watched warily as Storm lay down on
the old-fashioned bedspread and then
put his head on one side as if expecting
an answer.

'I'm Paige. Paige Riley. I'm staying in
this spooky old house because my
mum's in hospital resting until my baby
brother's born,' she found herself
explaining. 'My step-dad can't look after
me in our flat because he has to work.'

'I am honoured to meet you, Paige,'
Storm woofed, bowing his head.

Paige hardly dared to move in case
she frightened this amazing puppy away.

She noticed that Storm was beginning
to tremble all over.

'Are you OK?' Paige couldn't imagine
why he might be afraid of *her*.

'I need to hide. Can you help me?'
he whined.

Paige frowned. 'Who are you hiding
from? Is someone after you?'

Storm's bright blue eyes flashed with
anger and fear. 'Yes, a fierce lone wolf

called Shadow, who attacked my father and litter brothers and wounded my mother. Now he wants to lead the Moon-claw pack, but the others want me for their leader.'

Paige listened in amazement. 'But how can you lead a wolf pack? You're just a pup—' she began.

'I will show you!' Storm barked.

He jumped up and leapt off the bed on to the thick carpet. There was another dazzling bright gold flash, so bright that Paige was blinded for a moment.

'Oh!' she rubbed her eyes and when she could see again she realized that the cute Dalmatian puppy had disappeared. In its place, there stood a magnificent young silver-grey wolf.

Paige eyed the young wolf's sharp
teeth, muscular legs and huge paws that
seemed too big for his body. As he
shook himself, gold sparks danced out
of his thick fur. 'Storm?' she said,
inching back under the covers.

'Yes, it is me. Do not be afraid. I will
not harm you,' Storm rumbled in a
soft growl.

But before Paige had time to get used
to seeing Storm as his impressive real
self, a last flare of intense gold light
filled the gloomy bedroom and Storm
reappeared before her as a helpless little
Dalmatian puppy.

'Wow! You really are a wolf. No one
would ever guess,' Paige said, deeply
impressed by Storm's disguise.

'Shadow will not be fooled if he finds

me. I need to hide now.' Storm gave a
little whimper of fear as he began
trembling all over again.

Paige's soft heart went out to him.
With his smooth spotted fur, alert little
face and huge glowing blue eyes, Storm
was the most gorgeous puppy she had
ever seen. 'Why don't you jump back
up here and stay with me tonight?' she
suggested. 'This bed's so enormous that
half my school could hide in it. We can
think about what else to do in the
morning.'

Storm gave her a doggy grin and
then leapt back up on to the bed,
trailing gold sparks behind him like a
tiny comet. 'That is a good plan!'

Paige made a cosy bed for Storm by
fluffing up a spare pillow.

'Thank you, Paige,' Storm woofed.
He jumped on to the pillow and
circled round and round before finally
settling down. Tucking his nose between
his little spotted front paws, he gave a
contented sigh. 'This is a safe place.'

'Yes, but it's still very dark in here,'
Paige said, trying not to sound too
nervous.

Storm lifted his head again. Gold specks twinkled in his spotty fur and a soft glow spread outwards from him, lighting up the room. 'Is that better?'

'Much! Thanks, Storm.' Paige lay down and snuggled under the covers. The four-poster bed didn't seem so vast and lonely any more.

Maybe staying with Debs in this gloomy old house wouldn't be quite so bad now that she had Storm for a friend. As Paige and Storm fell asleep, the gentle glow filled every shadowy corner and just stopped short of spilling out under the door.

Chapter
THREE

'Rise and shine, darling!' Deborah
Stokes poked her head round the
bedroom door the following morning.
'Goodness me. Where did that puppy
come from? Keith didn't say anything
about you bringing a pet!'

Paige woke instantly. She sat up,
rubbing her eyes. Oh no. She must have
overslept!

Storm was just waking up too. He stretched his front paws out and yawned, showing a pink tongue and sharp little white teeth.

Debs put her hands on her hips. Her hair was loose on her shoulders and she was wearing a black kimono with big red poppies all over it. 'I'm waiting. I think you owe me an explanation, young lady,' she said sternly.

Paige gulped. 'You're never going to believe this, but Storm's here because he's hiding from his evil enemy. And guess what. He can ta—' she began excitedly, but Storm suddenly reached over and tapped her cheek with one tiny spotty front paw.

'Wroo-oof! Wroo-oof!' he said loudly, looking up at her with pleading

midnight-blue eyes and shaking his
head.

Paige looked at Storm, confused,
before realizing that the tiny puppy
didn't want her to tell Debs about him.
She patted him reassuringly, letting him
know that she understood.

'What's wrong with him? Why's he
making that noise?' Debs asked, puzzled.

'Um . . . I think Storm just woke up with a bit of a jolt. He was probably in the middle of a dream or something . . .' Paige improvised hastily. She began wracking her brains for something more convincing to tell Debs that would protect Storm's secret. 'Sorry, I got a bit carried away. What I meant to say was that I'm . . . er, looking after Storm for a . . . friend. But I haven't told Mum or Keith about it. I was going to hide him in my bedroom at the flat, but then Mum was taken to hospital and I had to come here. Storm was in my . . . um . . . shoulder bag when Keith drove me here last night and I smuggled him upstairs. I just really want him to stay! I was going to buy dog food with my pocket money,' she fibbed.

'Hmm,' Debs said doubtfully. 'Why can't your friend look after her own puppy?'

'Oh, she can . . . when . . . when she gets back from her holiday,' Paige rushed on, thinking that this was getting very complicated. 'But pets aren't allowed in their hotel and all the boarding kennels were full. That's why I said I'd look after him.'

Debs stood for a moment in silence before reaching out to stroke Storm. Storm looked up at her with big dewy eyes and gave a little whine. He wagged his tail and licked her hand.

Paige had to smile at his 'Please-like-me-and-let-me-stay' act.

It worked. Debs's face softened. 'He's certainly a cute little chap and he seems friendly, but I hadn't banked on having a puppy around. I'm very proud of my garden. I really don't want him digging up holes in my flowerbeds and burying bones.'

'Oh, he wouldn't do that!' Paige promised. 'I'll make sure Storm behaves himself. Please say that he can stay with me. And . . . and you won't tell Keith

about this, will you?' she asked in her best pleading voice. 'I'll be grounded for at least a year!'

Debs looked at her sternly and then a big grin stole over her face. 'You're a cheeky minx and no mistake! But I admire people who show initiative. All right, Storm can stay. And he'll be our secret.'

'Really? That's brilliant! Thanks *so* much,' Paige cried. 'I'll look after him really well. You'll hardly notice he's here.'

Debs nodded. 'See that you do,' she said firmly, her eyes twinkling.

Downstairs, Debs cooked them all a breakfast of sausages, eggs and toast. She even let Paige give Storm two sausages,

cut into tiny pieces. 'But only until we
get some proper dog food. I don't want
him being sick on my antique carpets,'
she commented.

Paige thought that you'd hardly
notice, they were so covered in swirls
and patterns, but she wisely kept silent.
After they finished eating, she took
Storm into the garden to have a little
run around.

'I'm actually starting to quite like Debs,' she said, wandering after him in case any of Debs's flowers got trampled by little paws. 'She seems strict, but she's kind too.'

'I like her as well,' Storm woofed in agreement and then his little face turned serious. 'Thank you for not telling her my secret. You can never tell anyone; promise me, Paige.'

Paige felt disappointed. She thought Storm might say this but had secretly been hoping she could tell Amy and Tori all about her magical new friend. They would think this was so cool! Paige was prepared to do whatever it took to keep Storm safe though. 'OK. I promise. No one's going to hear about you from me – ever!'

Storm wrinkled his little pink muzzle and black nose, rolled his lips back and showed his teeth. Paige blinked, worried that Storm was snarling. But he wasn't making growling noises. Why was he doing that?

Storm looked surprised at himself. He did it again. 'Oh, this is how I show that I am pleased. It is a smile. It is something special that Dalmatian dogs do,' he yapped.

Paige felt a laugh bubbling up inside her, but she didn't want to hurt his feelings. Storm looked as cute as could be, sitting there practising his Dalmatian grin.

A moment later he shot across the lawn to chase some leaves that were whirling about in the breeze.

Paige watched him affectionately. She loved having Storm all to herself and not having to share him with anyone.

Chapter
FOUR

Keith came over to pick Paige up that
afternoon before he went to the factory.
'I thought you'd like to visit your
mum,' he said. 'It might cheer her up.
She's already bored with having to rest
in bed.'

Paige smiled. She'd known she
would be.

'How are you and Debs getting on?'

Keith asked anxiously as they stood in
the hall.

'Fine,' Paige said, shrugging. 'I don't
even mind staying with her, as long as
it's not for too long.'

Keith looked pleased. 'I'm glad, Paige.
That'll be a big relief for your mum,
and I really think Debs is enjoying your
company.'

He ruffled her short brown hair

fondly and went off to have a quick
chat with Debs, while Paige went
upstairs to get ready.

Paige found Storm dozing on her
bed. With the autumn sunlight pouring
through the window on to him, his
dark spots really showed up against his
smooth white fur. He opened one
bright blue eye and wagged his tail as
Paige bent over him.

'Will you be OK here all by
yourself until I get back from town?'
she asked.

Storm's other eye snapped open and
he sprang up on to his paws. 'I will
come with you!' he woofed eagerly.

Paige smiled and stroked the top of
his silky head. 'I'd love you to. But
what if Keith sees you? Besides, I

don't think puppies are allowed in hospitals.'

'I will use my magic so that no one but you will be able to see and hear me,' Storm told her.

'You can make yourself invisible? Cool! There's no problem then. Maybe you should still get into my shoulder bag? You'll be safer in there until we get to the hospital.'

Paige unzipped her bag and Storm jumped in and settled down on top of her woolly gloves. After brushing her hair and pulling on a fleece body warmer, Paige picked up her bag and went downstairs to where Keith was waiting.

They said goodbye to Debs and then headed for the hospital. Paige suggested they stop on the way to buy some magazines. 'Mum likes the celebrity gossip ones,' she told him.

'Good idea. I'll get her some flowers too,' Keith said.

At the hospital, he showed Paige down the maze of corridors to the maternity ward. Paige spotted her mum right away. She was sitting up on the second bed from the entrance.

Mrs Riley's eyes lit up when she saw Keith and Paige. She looked flushed and pretty in a new blue nightdress and matching dressing gown.

Paige rushed over to give her mum a hug and a kiss, delighted to see her looking well.

'Ooh, flowers *and* magazines. Lovely. You two are spoiling me!' her mum exclaimed.

Paige sat down on the visitor's chair beside the bed. 'You deserve to be spoiled, Mum. Are you OK?'

'I'm a bit tired, but that's all. I feel like a bit of a fraud staying in here actually,' her mum replied, pulling a face. She patted her round tummy. 'I'll be glad when this little man makes his appearance!'

Paige chose not to say anything. She slipped her bag off her shoulder to put it on the floor and saw Storm jump out and go gambling off down the ward. He had his head down, and his tail was wagging as he snuffed up the interesting smells. Even though Paige knew that the tiny spotty puppy was invisible to everyone else, she still expected a nurse or someone to notice him. But when

nothing happened, she began to relax.
Storm was much less trouble than a
baby brother was going to be!

'I'll go and see if I can find a vase to
put these flowers in. You girls can have
a good old natter,' Keith said.

'He's being tactful,' Mrs Riley
commented. 'I hope it's not too awful
in that loopy old house with Debs. She

used to be an actress, you know. And she still dresses like one! Is she bossing you around or anything? Just let me know and I'll have a word with her.'

Paige grinned at the determined look on her mum's face. 'Debs has actually been really nice to me and St–' She stopped herself quickly, realizing that she would have to be a lot more careful about keeping Storm's secret. 'But I'm not keen on all her antique stuff. You should see the monster bed I'm sleeping in! It's as big as the entire kitchen in our flat!'

'Well, don't get used to having all that space to yourself,' her mum said, laughing. 'You'll have to go back to your ordinary poky old bedroom.'

'I like my bedroom being small. It's

cosy,' Paige said. 'But I can put up with staying away from home for a little bit longer, I guess.'

'Well, I'm glad you're making the best of things. Don't say anything to Keith, but I was worried that you'd feel a bit lonely and cut off over in Brookton, what with Debs having no car.'

'Oh, I'll manage,' Paige said. *I'm not lonely, now that I've got Storm for my friend*, she thought. She could see him sniffing around under the bed opposite. Her lips twitched as she imagined the look on her mum's face if she knew there was an invisible puppy a few metres away!

Mrs Riley reached out and took Paige's hand. 'I'm sorry that your birthday's going to be a bit of a non-event with me in here. Keith obviously can't manage a party with the hours he's working. You don't mind too much, do you, pet?'

Paige minded very much. She swallowed. 'No problem, Mum. There's always next year,' she said, trying hard to hide her disappointment.

'That's my lovely sensible good girl. I knew you'd understand,' her mum said, fondly squeezing her hand. 'Once I get

home we'll have some serious girl time all to ourselves; all right?'

Paige nodded, but she couldn't make herself believe it. The lady in the flat next door had a baby. It hardly seemed to sleep at all and when it was awake it was crying to be fed or changed.

A lump rose in her throat as she wished that she could have her mum all to herself again, like before she met Keith and before a baby half-brother was on its way. Paige felt a pang as she realized that she wasn't ready to get into the big sister thing.

'Had a good chat, you two?' Keith said, putting the vase of flowers on top of the bedside cabinet.

Paige nodded and managed a wobbly smile. While her mum and Keith were talking, she leafed through one of her mum's magazines. Storm padded over, lay down and rested his front paws on one of her trainers.

'Is something wrong?' he woofed.

Paige checked that no one was listening before she replied. 'I'm just feeling a bit fed up, that's all,' she whispered.

'Can I do anything to help?' Storm offered.

Paige shook her head. 'No one can.' But as she looked into his bright midnight-blue eyes, she felt herself cheering up a bit. At least Storm was here just for her.

Keith dropped Paige and Storm at Debs's house and then left for work

straightaway. There was a note from
Debs in the kitchen, saying that she was
at her book group at a friend's house
down the road and wouldn't be long.
She'd scribbled a phone number too, if
Paige needed it.

Paige got herself a drink and forked
some dog food into a bowl for Storm.
Storm chomped it up and then sat
back, licking his chops. He trotted over
to the table where Paige was sitting,
staring glumly into her orange juice.

'You are very quiet, Paige,' he woofed,
his blue eyes clouding with concern.

Paige sighed heavily. 'I was thinking
about not having a birthday party this
year. It's not fair. And I don't even
know what to do about Amy and Tori.
I know they'd understand about Mum

51

being in hospital. But I'd feel really
weird about going to their parties, if
they can't come to mine. Maybe I
should just phone and say that I'm not
coming.'

'Then your friends would be upset
too,' Storm woofed.

Paige realized that he was right. 'I
wouldn't want that. OK, maybe I'll still
go. Amy's is on Friday. That's only the
day after tomorrow and I haven't got
her a present yet. I should have got her
one while I was with Keith. Now it's
too late. The buses into town from here
only run about once every ten years!'

Storm's midnight-blue eyes lit up
with purpose. 'I will help. Put me
down, please.'

Paige did so. She frowned as she felt

a strange warm tingling sensation
flowing down her spine as bright gold
sparks began igniting in Storm's smooth
spotty fur.

Something very unusual was about to
happen.

Chapter
FIVE

Paige watched in complete amazement
as the sparks in Storm's fur grew
brighter and brighter and his ears
crackled and popped with electricity.
A glowing gold light spread around
them both. It began forming into a
long glittery tube that suddenly
whooshed through the kitchen
window.

Paige stared at the shining rainbow-shaped tube as it seemed to come to rest somewhere in the region of the town. In the middle of Debs's kitchen, there was now an entrance to a hollow tunnel. Its walls were made of millions of swirly sparks, linked together like chain mail.

'Follow me, Paige,' Storm barked, leaping into the tunnel-tube.

'Wait for me!' Paige called a second later, dashing after him.

The magic tunnel was springy underfoot and the walls rippled, bouncing Paige along, so that in no time at all she suddenly shot out with a loud *Pop!* Storm sat on the pavement, waiting for her.

'Oh! That was fantastic!' Paige gasped, swaying slightly. Her legs felt quite wobbly — just like she'd been on a bouncy castle!

She looked around and saw that she and Storm were now in a quiet alleyway behind some wheelie bins. Paige realized where they were. There was a big shopping centre just round the corner.

'Now you can buy Amy a present,'

Storm woofed, looking pleased with himself.

Paige quickly bent down to stroke him. 'Thanks, Storm.'

She didn't waste any time, as they had to get back before Debs returned and noticed they were both gone. Paige hurried into a big store and went straight to the toy department. Amy was mad about fairies and had heaps of fairy books. She even had a string of fairy lights around her wall mirror.

Paige chose a fairy dolly with a lavender dress and crown and matching glittery wings. 'Perfect! Isn't she pretty?' she whispered to Storm. 'Have I got time to get a card?'

'Yes, but you will have to hurry. This

sort of magic does not last long,' Storm barked softly.

Paige set off again, but on reaching the card department she stared in dismay. 'There're about a hundred million cards here. I don't know which one to choose.'

Storm waved one tiny front paw and a shower of golden glitter shot out. From out of the corner of her eye, Paige noticed a fairy-shaped card glowing as brightly as a star on one of the racks. As she picked it up and opened it, tinkling fairy music played 'Happy Birthday'.

'Yay! Amy will love this!' Paige went and paid and then hurried outside into the alleyway after the little puppy.

The golden tube began to fade as

Paige got close. There was no time to waste. She and Storm plunged in and once again, Paige felt the tunnel's springy walls and floor helping them along.

Suddenly, the tube began to ripple much faster than before and Paige and Storm went shooting forward.

'Ooer!' she cried as, with a loud burping noise, the tunnel spat them

both out and they landed on their
bottoms on the kitchen floor. The
tunnel began to dissolve into fizzing
sparks before disappearing with a final
loud *Pop!*

Paige gingerly picked herself up and
grinned. 'That was so much fun and
I've got a brilliant present for Amy.
Thank you, Storm!'

The tiny puppy's little muzzle
wrinkled in his cute Dalmatian grin.
'I am glad I was able to help.'

Paige had barely caught her breath,
when the kitchen door swung open
and Debs came in.

'Hello, darling. Discussing all those
books has made me hungry. I think it's
time for dinner. Have you and Storm
been having a good time?' she asked.

'Er . . . yeah!' Paige said, winking at the tiny puppy. *You'd never believe me, even if I told you*, she thought.

On Friday, Debs insisted on booking a taxi, so Paige and Storm arrived in style at Amy's house. Storm was invisible, to save Paige having to offer awkward explanations.

'Happy Birthday!' Paige gave Amy her card and present.

Tori stood by as Amy unwrapped it. 'Oh, I absolutely love her!' Amy said delightedly, clutching her lavender fairy doll. 'How did you know?'

'Know what?' Paige asked, puzzled.

Amy and Tori exchanged knowing glances. 'Come and see!' They practically hauled Paige into the kitchen.

Paige's eyes widened as she saw the
pink tablecloth strewn with sequins,
the plates of dainty food and the big
birthday cake in the shape of a fairy
castle. There were sparkly pink and
violet streamers trailing down the walls.

'It's a *total* fairy party! Don't you just
love it?' Amy said.

'Wow! It looks . . . magical!' Paige
said delightedly.

They played Pin the Wing on the
Fairy. Everyone fell about laughing
when Amy's dad pinned the wing on
the fairy's nose. There was Pass the
Magic Parcel and then a dressing–up
game with cardboard, tinsel and
coloured tissue and a prize for the best
fairy costume. Tori won it easily.

'Wait until you see what we're doing

at *my* party,' Tori said to Paige. 'It's going to be very grown-up. Fairies are OK, but they're a bit babyish, aren't they?' she said, flicking back her long hair.

'Amy doesn't seem to think so. Neither do I,' Paige replied. 'Aren't you having fun?'

'Well – yes,' Tori admitted.

'What are you moaning about then, you muppet!' Paige joked, giving her a friendly dig in the ribs.

Tori laughed. 'It's so great that our birthdays are so close together, isn't it? We're the Party Girls!' she said, doing a twirl.

Not this year, Paige thought sadly, but she didn't want to spoil the happy mood by saying anything yet.

When no one was watching, Paige
gave Storm some party treats. He sat on
the window sill, enjoying watching the
party without being trodden on. 'I like
party food,' he woofed happily,
chomping his fairy-sized sandwiches
and crisps.

When Paige's taxi arrived to take her
home, Amy's mum handed her a pink
satin goody bag. Paige said her thank
yous and goodbyes and Amy and Tori
waved from the doorstep. 'See you at
my party on Monday!' Tori called.

Storm sat on Paige's lap in the back
of the taxi. 'I don't mind going back to
Debs's too much. I'm starting to quite
like her,' Paige sighed, stroking his soft
spotty fur. 'But it feels mega-wrong
not to have a party. Especially as me,

Amy and Tori have spent ages talking about it.'

Storm whined sympathetically.

Debs was waiting eagerly at the door to let Paige and Storm in. 'Tell me everything and don't leave anything out! What did your friends say when they saw Storm? Did you tell them you were looking after a puppy?'

'Um, yes. They made a big fuss of

Storm,' Paige said. She quickly changed the subject. 'Amy's party had a fairy theme. It looked so pretty . . .' she said.

Debs listened as Paige told her about the games and the yummy party food. 'I've been thinking,' she said when Paige had finished. 'It's a shame that you can't celebrate your birthday properly with your mum in hospital. How would you like a tea party here, for you, Amy and Tori?'

'Really?' Paige said, surprised. She hadn't the heart to tell Debs that she'd been looking forward to something a bit more special. A tea party didn't sound all that exciting. 'Thanks very much. That would be . . . very nice.'

Debs beamed. 'That's settled then.'

Chapter
SIX

The next time Keith took Paige and
Storm to the hospital to visit her mum,
she made sure she asked him to take
her shopping afterwards.

'OK then. But I'm in a bit of a rush.
Do you know which shop you need?'
Keith said.

Paige nodded. She knew just what
Tori wanted. She bought her a CD of

her favourite boy band, a pack of
coloured gel pens and a card in the
shape of a shiny designer handbag. 'And
can we just pop back to the flat? I want
to get some clothes. I'll be super-quick!'
she pleaded.

Keith drove to their block and sat
outside with the engine running, while
Paige dashed up the stairs and along the
concrete walkway. Storm followed Paige
into her bedroom and flopped down on
her fluffy floor cushion while she
burrowed in the wardrobe.

'I like this place,' he woofed, looking
around at the bright posters on the
walls.

'Me too! It's tiny but it's all mine,'
Paige said, stuffing a blue top with a
sparkly butterfly and her newest jeans

into her bag. It felt comforting being back home among her snow domes, framed pictures and old Barbie dolls. She couldn't resist picking up the battered old teddy who always sat on her bed and giving him a cuddle.

When it was time to go, she had to wrench herself away. She sighed sadly as she shouldered her bag and quickly locked the front door. 'I wish I didn't

have to go back to Debs. I can't wait until mum comes home and we can be a family again,' she said to Storm as they hurried back down to where Keith was waiting.

Only now, it'll be a different kind of family, she thought worriedly. *One with a tiny smelly fussy baby that demands everyone's attention.*

On Monday night, Paige dressed in her sparkly butterfly top and jeans.

'Oh, you do look pretty. Wait a minute, I've got just the thing to go with that outfit,' Debs said.

Paige pulled a face. 'Oh no. She's probably going to bring me one of her flowing velvet jackets,' she whispered to Storm.

'Is that a bad thing?' Storm woofed
softly, looking puzzled.

'Er . . . yes!' Paige said. 'I can hardly
go out looking like a pair of curtains!'

But Debs returned with a pair of neat
clip-on earrings, the same colour blue
as Paige's top. Paige put them on. 'Oh,
I love them! Thanks, Debs. They're
perfect.'

Debs looked pleased. 'Would you like me to do your hair? I've got a set of heated rollers somewhere.'

Paige was thinking how to refuse politely, not wanting to push her luck, when Amy and her mum arrived to pick her up.

'Have a good time,' Debs called as Paige walked down the front garden. 'Oh, just a minute. Haven't you forgotten something? Storm!'

Paige froze. Storm was walking invisibly at her ankles. Debs obviously couldn't see him, so she thought Paige had left him behind. Turning round, she ran back towards Debs. 'I left him in my room. He seemed a bit tired,' she said, hoping Debs wouldn't go upstairs to check.

'What was all that about?' Amy asked as Paige got into the back seat of the car and sat next to her. 'She said something about a storm.'

'Um . . . yes. She thought it might rain later . . .' Paige said vaguely. 'Anyway, don't let's worry about that. We've got Tori's brother Dean to worry about instead. Yuk! I hope he isn't at the party − he's a real pain.'

'You can say that again,' Amy said.

'He's a real pain,' Paige repeated and they both laughed.

When they arrived at Tori's house, Paige spotted a tall thin boy with dark hair and a pimply face. 'Oh great. There's Dean,' she whispered to Storm. 'Look out for him. He can be a real nuisance with his nasty jokes.'

Storm showed his teeth in a tiny growl. 'That is not a good way to act.'

Amy, Paige and Storm wandered into the bright shiny kitchen and gave Tori her presents. There was a big display of expensive gifts on a sideboard. 'Those are all mine. Aren't I lucky?' Tori said proudly.

'Well, you are our bestest sweetest big girl,' her mum cooed, giving her a hug.

Dean pretended to stick his finger in his mouth and made gagging movements. For once, Paige didn't blame him. But then he spoiled it by hanging around and making stupid comments while Tori opened her presents. 'Felt tips! Bor-ring. You're ten, not six, aren't you?' he hooted, when she opened Paige's.

Paige blushed hotly, as she felt Storm nudge her leg protectively with his wet little nose.

Tori just giggled. 'They're gel pens actually. Just what I wanted. And this CD is great. Thanks, Paige.'

'That's OK,' Paige said, glaring at Dean and wishing he'd clear off.

Dean pulled a face at her and sloped out of the kitchen.

'This way, everyone!' Tori cried, leading the way into the sitting room.

The two enormous leather sofas had been pushed back and a shiny covering placed over the carpet to make a dance floor. A stack of disco equipment with big speakers stood near a row of lights flashing different colours.

Paige and Amy were seriously

impressed. 'Wow! It's just like a proper club!' Amy said.

Tori smiled proudly. 'I *told* you I was having a grown-up party. I'll put the CD Paige bought on my new player and we can do our routine to it.'

Paige felt self-conscious with everyone watching. But she soon relaxed and remembered all the steps. Everyone clapped when they finished.

Storm barked excitedly too, but only Paige could hear him. She winked at him when no one was looking.

The dancing was great fun, until Dean joined in. He jumped about, knocking into people on purpose.

'Ow!' Paige cried, when he leapt on her foot. 'Now who's acting like a six-year-old!' she muttered crossly.

Dean's face darkened as he heard her. 'Listen, everyone! Paige's in a rage! I'm really scared,' he mocked.

'You're so pathetic,' Paige said disgustedly, turning her back.

Tori's dad made fruit-juice cocktails with coloured ice cubes and little umbrellas. He handed them round on a tray, like a real waiter. 'Food's ready, when you've finished dancing,' he announced.

Storm followed Paige outside to the super-sized barbecue. His little black nose twitched at the delicious smells wafting towards him. 'That human food smells good,' he woofed.

Paige smiled at him. 'Knowing Tori's parents, there'll be millions of posh sausages and top-notch burgers. You'll love them.'

Everyone trooped over to the tables and chairs on the lawn. Storm sat under Paige's table. She slipped him some meat, but he found plenty to chomp up from all the bits the others dropped. It was all Paige could do not to giggle. He was better than a vacuum cleaner!

'My party's the best in the whole world, isn't it? Wait until you see my cake. It's got three layers *and* sugar roses.

The bottom's chocolate, the middle's lemon and the top's strawberry. It's mega-lush,' Tori said.

Paige fought down a stab of anxiety. Debs's tea party idea was looking more pale and pathetic by the moment. Maybe she should just tell Debs that she didn't want a party after all. Amy and Tori were going to be so disappointed with a dull old tea party.

Paige shook her head sadly as Tori's mum lit the candles on the amazing birthday cake and everyone sang 'Happy Birthday'. Paige took a plate when the multi-coloured slices were handed round, but she didn't feel very hungry any more.

Soon afterwards, parents began arriving to pick up their kids.

'Mum will be here for us soon. I'm going to get my coat,' Amy said.

'OK,' Paige replied. She decided that she'd better fetch Storm. The last time she'd seen him he was exploring the bottom of the garden.

But Paige couldn't find him. He definitely wasn't nosing about in any of the flower beds. Suddenly, a loud yelp of fear came from the direction of the tree house.

Paige gasped as she caught sight of the tiny spotted puppy wobbling on a branch, high above the ground!

Chapter
SEVEN

Paige's pulse raced as she ran towards the tree.

'Come back here, you stupid mutt!' a voice called angrily and Paige saw Dean leaning out of the tree-house window, reaching for the trembling puppy.

Paige realized that Storm must be so scared that he'd forgotten to make himself invisible. He couldn't use his magic to help himself now that Dean could see him.

'Hang on, Storm!' Paige cried as she leapt forward. Suddenly, Storm's paws slipped and his back legs swung in mid-air. His tiny legs scrabbled for a foothold and then he whimpered as he felt himself falling.

Paige's heart missed a beat. She

stretched out her arms and just
managed to catch Storm, but she was
still rushing forward. With the tiny
puppy in her arms, she couldn't put out
her hands to stop herself and crashed
into the tree trunk with a massive *thud*.

Paige fell to the ground, dazed.

'Oh, flipping heck!' Dean cried. He
ducked inside the tree house and began
climbing down.

Paige felt a familiar prickling
sensation down her spine as bright gold
sparks bloomed in Storm's spotty fur
and his little black nose glowed like a
gold nugget. Storm leaned close and
very gently touched her chin with the
tip of his wet nose.

A warm fizzing feeling spread
outwards from Paige's chin. It washed

over her face and forehead and then
trickled down over the back of her
neck. In just a second she felt as
clear-headed as if she'd just eaten a
very strong peppermint.

She sat up with Storm still in her lap.

Dean appeared beside them, just as
every last spark faded from Storm's coat.

'You're sitting up! I thought you –' he
said in a panicky voice.

'We're fine. No thanks to you!' Paige
fumed, losing her temper. 'What sort of
person tries to scare a tiny puppy,
especially high up in a tree!'

'I didn't mean to scare him!' Dean
snapped, flushing. 'I was just mucking
around.' His eyes narrowed. 'How come
you know its name, anyway? Is it yours?
I didn't see you with it at the party.'

Paige hesitated. 'I've . . . um . . . seen Storm around here before. He must live with one of your neighbours.'

'Funny. I've never seen him,' Dean said suspiciously. 'I'll come with you to take him back.'

'No! I mean, I can do it by myself,' Paige insisted, but her heart sank as she saw the determined look on Dean's face.

As Dean took a step towards Paige, Storm lifted his lip and growled softly. He leapt out of her lap and ran behind the tree.

Paige felt another faint tingling sensation down her spine. A little spurt of gold sparks puffed up from a nearby pile of grass cuttings and vegetable peelings. Suddenly, there was a strong gust of breeze, which blew the entire heap towards Dean.

Whoosh! A cascade of compost swept him off his feet. *Splop!* It covered Dean up to his neck and held him firmly to the ground. 'Help!' he croaked, spitting out shreds of brownish leaves.

Paige left him there. 'You'd better stay invisible now. Come on, Amy's mum's probably here to pick us up,' she

whispered to Storm as they hurried back towards the house. 'What you did to Dean was a bit naughty,' she scolded gently. 'But he deserved it!'

Storm's bright blue eyes glowed with mischief. He wrinkled his muzzle in a cute Dalmatian grin. 'Perhaps it will teach that mean boy a lesson. My magic will wear off in a few minutes.'

Paige laughed. 'I'd give two weeks' pocket money to see him trying to explain how a compost heap attacked him! Brothers definitely seem like a real pain.'

Storm put his head on one side. 'But having a baby brother might be different. He would be little and helpless and it would be someone to look after,' he woofed softly.

'Maybe,' Paige said, not convinced.

She felt a surge of affection for the tiny puppy. She knew that Storm meant well and didn't want to hurt his feelings by disagreeing. But she was still very far from being happy about having to share her mum with the baby.

A couple of evenings later, Paige and Debs sat on the dark blue velvet sofa with Storm curled up between them. They were watching a late-night TV film about some kids who got trapped in a haunted house.

'I'm not sure your mum would approve. Maybe we should switch channels before this film gives you nightmares,' Debs said, reaching for the remote.

'Oh, I watch much worse stuff than this,' Paige fibbed. She felt very grown up, staying up late and eating popcorn with Debs. Besides, nothing could scare her while she was cuddled up in bed with Storm!

She reached down to stroke his smooth warm little body. On the TV, a door in the haunted house creaked open, revealing a four-poster bed and heavy furniture. Storm pricked up his ears and sat straight.

'Groof!' he barked, pawing Paige's arm excitedly. 'Why is your bedroom in that box with moving pictures?'

Paige grinned. It did look just like her bedroom. She'd always thought this house was the perfect setting for a creepy film!

A brilliant idea for a birthday party
jumped into her mind. She was dying
to tell Storm about it now, but she
daren't risk it with Debs sitting so
close.

As soon as the film finished, Paige
jumped up and went into the kitchen
to make Debs a cup of tea. She piled
some biscuits on to a plate and brought
them back in with the tea. She saw that

Storm wasn't on the sofa and decided to go and look for him after she'd spoken to Debs.

'Ooh, lovely. Thanks,' Debs said, taking a sip of tea. 'What have I done to deserve this? Are you after something, young lady?' she joked.

Paige felt herself blushing. 'Well . . . actually, I did want to talk to you about my . . . um . . . birthday tea party,' she said sheepishly.

Debs dunked a ginger nut. 'Fire away then. I'm all ears.'

'I was wondering if Tori and Amy could stay the night. Instead of a tea party, maybe we could have a midnight feast. We could easily all sleep in my bed. I thought we could read ghost stories and play creepy games. It could be a scary sleepover. What do you think?' she asked.

Debs nodded thoughtfully and beamed at Paige. 'You clever old thing, you! I wish I'd thought of it. It's a great idea. I've got some old Halloween decorations in the attic and we could put some candles in glass jam jars. I'll dress up and be your spooky waitress, if you like. How about if I made dead man's hands, skeleton biscuits and blood tablets for the midnight feast?' she said, getting into the swing of things.

'Ooh, yes! That would be fantastic!' Paige cried delightedly. 'Can I help make them?'

'Course you can. That's half the fun. There's a bus into town tomorrow. We can go shopping, if you like. I was going to ask if you wanted to come with me and choose a present. And we could pop and visit your mum if we've got time. What do you think?'

'Yay! Thanks, Debs. You're the best!' Paige threw her arms round Debs and hugged her. She couldn't wait to find Storm and tell him her exciting news.

Chapter
EIGHT

Paige skipped upstairs, expecting to see
the tiny puppy curled up on her bed,
but he was nowhere in sight. 'Storm?'
she said, looking around the room.

She checked under the pillows and
covers and then looked under the bed
and in the wardrobe. But there was still
no sign of Storm. Paige finally found
him underneath the old-fashioned

dressing table, curled into a tight ball against the wall.

'Oh, I get it. We're playing hide-and-seek —' Paige began and then her face changed as she saw that the tiny puppy was trembling. 'What's wrong? Are you sick?'

Storm shook his head, his midnight-blue eyes troubled. 'I sensed that Shadow was close and I heard dogs growling in the street outside the house. I think he has set them on to me,' he whimpered.

Paige felt a stir of alarm, but she hadn't heard anything with the TV on. She went and peered through a crack in the curtains, but the street below was empty. 'There aren't any dogs there now,' she told him. 'How will I know they're Shadow's dogs if they come back?'

Storm lifted his head. 'They will be ordinary dogs, with fierce pale eyes and extra-long sharp teeth. Shadow's magic will make any dog I meet into my enemy now.'

'Then we'll have to make sure that you keep well hidden,' Paige said. She managed to reach right underneath the dressing table with one hand and stroke Storm reassuringly.

The terrified puppy slowly uncurled

and finally crept out with his belly
brushing against the carpet. Paige
picked him up and gently tucked him
into bed. 'There, you're safe now. I hope
that horrible Shadow will keep right on
going and fall into the sea! Then you
can stay with me forever and live in
our flat,' she said.

Storm peeped over the covers, his
little face serious. 'I cannot do that.
One day I must return to my own
world and the Moon-claw pack. Do
you understand that, Paige?' he
woofed.

Paige nodded sadly but she didn't
want to think about that now. She
loved having Storm all to herself.
Climbing on to the bed, she curled
herself round Storm.

'I've just been talking to Debs. I've got some great news about my party . . .'

Paige grinned at the squeals of delight coming down the phone the following day when she told Amy and Tori about her party. They were both at Tori's house listening to CDs.

'A scary sleepover is so cool!' Amy said.

'Yes. Almost as good as my party,' Tori said.

'See you both on Saturday! And remember to bring your PJs.' Paige replaced the phone before turning to Storm. 'I'm going into town with Debs now. I'd love you to come with us, but I'm worried about Shadow finding you.'

'I am too,' Storm barked, his bright eyes flickering with fear. 'You go with Debs and I will stay here and hide.'

'OK then, if you're sure. See you later. We'll bring you a treat back,' Paige promised.

Although she had a lovely day with Debs in town, she couldn't help feeling anxious. What if Storm's enemies came back? He might have to leave without even saying goodbye. The thought of Storm leaving made her realize how much she adored her magical friend. She felt determined to enjoy every precious moment with him.

'Would you like something to wear for your birthday?' Debs asked. They were on the way back to the bus stop

with bulging carrier bags and had
stopped outside a clothes shop.

'OK,' Paige said, hiding her
impatience for Debs's sake. Inside the
shop, she dashed up to the first rack
and grabbed a black-and-silver top in
her size. 'Can I have this, please?'

Debs raised her eyebrows. 'Don't you
want to try it on?'

'No. This size fits me fine. I love it. It's just right for my sleepover.'

'All right. If you're sure,' Debs said. She paid for the top and they set off for the bus.

It was only half an hour later, but to Paige it felt like hours before the bus dropped them at the bottom of the lane in Brookton. The moment they got in the house, she dumped her carrier bag in the kitchen and shot upstairs.

'I need the loo!' she shouted over her shoulder at a surprised Debs.

As soon as she went into the bedroom, Paige saw Storm's little spotty tail sticking out from under one of the pillows. 'I'm back. Storm!' she crooned happily, gently uncovering him. She picked him up and cuddled him,

breathing in his clean puppy smell. 'I'm
so glad that you're still here! My scary
sleepover party wouldn't be any fun
without you.'

'I am looking forward to that very
much,' Storm yapped, his pink tongue
darting out as he covered her chin and
nose in warm little licks.

'Happy Birthday, love!' Mrs Riley said,
handing Paige her card and presents.

As Paige opened them, her face lit up.
She had some new trainers, a Hunt the
Monster board game and a gift card for
downloading music. 'Wow! Thanks.
These are brilliant!' she said, hugging
her mum and then Keith.

Storm sat beneath the visitor's chair.
As there'd been no more sign of any

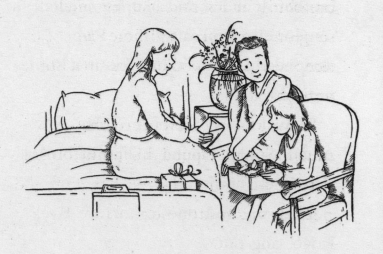

enemy dogs, he and Paige had decided
that it was safe for him to come too.

At the end of visiting time, Paige
kissed her mum. Paige thought she
looked a bit pale. 'Are you OK?' she
asked her.

'Yes, fine. Your brother's a bit restless,
that's all.'

Paige remembered what Storm had
said to her about having a new little

brother. It did sound like he needed someone to look after him. Paige decided that she'd think about it some more later on.

'Have a lovely sleepover party, pet. And I wouldn't mind a slice of birthday cake!' her mum said.

'I'll bring you one tomorrow. Bye!' Paige sang out.

Chapter
NINE

Paige and Debs worked flat out, getting things ready for the party. Paige helped decorate gingerbread men biscuits with black-and-white icing for skeletons. The blood tablets turned out to be tiny strawberry-jam sandwiches. But the dead man's hands were her favourites.

'These are dead clever. Dead, get it!'

Paige joked, filling clear plastic food
gloves with popcorn, before tying the
ends and dipping the finger tips into
pink icing.

Debs laughed. 'That's a truly terrible
joke.'

Paige smiled at Storm, who was
'helping' by crunching up any bits of
popcorn that escaped. Time seemed to
fly and Paige had to run upstairs to get
changed.

She had just thrown on her new
black-and-silver top, when the doorbell
rang. Paige came downstairs, with
Storm at her heels to let her friends in.

Amy beamed at Storm as he wagged
his tail in a friendly fashion. 'Oh, what
a cute puppy! Is he yours?' she said,
fussing over him.

Tori bent down to stroke Storm too.
'Was he a present for your birthday?
You never said you were getting a
puppy. What's he called?'

'Storm,' Paige said. 'He's . . . er . . .
not mine. I'm just looking after him for
someone while I'm staying here. Debs
has been great about it.'

'Did someone mention my name?'
called a deep hollow voice. Debs glided
into the hall, wearing flowing black
clothes. Her face was milk white and
her mouth was a slash of red. 'I am
Paige's witchy godmother and I am at
your service for tonight! This way,
please!'

Paige was impressed. Debs was very
convincing. She must have been a really
good actress.

Amy and Tori's eyes widened in delight when they saw the party food. The dead man's hands were a huge success. The birthday cake was an extra surprise from Debs. It was shaped into a monster face, with sugared jelly-worm hair, a liquorice nose and eyebrows and gobstopper eyeballs.

Debs made a magic potion by

scooping ice cream into glasses of cola
before handing them round.

Paige loved her presents. Amy's was a
comedy DVD called *Revenge of the
Monster Moles*. Tori had bought her an
expensive-looking notebook and
matching folder and some sparkly hair
slides.

'Your chamber is ready, young ladies,
if you'd like to follow me upstairs,' Debs
said in her spooky voice.

'I can't wait to see their faces when
they see my room,' Paige whispered to
Storm.

Plastic bats and spiders hung from the
ceiling. Red-and-black streamers and
fake spiders' webs decorated the bed,
and candles glowed from inside jam
jars on the window sill.

'I can*not* believe that bed!' Tori jumped on to it and lay spread out like a starfish. 'Come on. Let's get our PJs on!'

They all undressed and got into bed. Even with three girls and a puppy in the bed, there was still heaps of room. Storm curled up on the pillow next to Paige. Tori and Amy made a huge fuss of him.

'I wish I had a puppy like yours,' Tori crooned. 'I'm going to make my mum and dad buy me one exactly like Storm,' she decided.

Paige bit back a grin. 'I think they'd have a job. Storm's one of a kind,' she said, smiling fondly at him.

Tori looked a teeny bit put out. 'He's not the only Dalmatian puppy in the world, you know,' she said huffily.

'You're so lucky, Paige,' Amy said. 'Debs is great and you can stay in this amazing house whenever you like. And you're going to have a sweet little baby brother soon.'

'I wish I had a young brother or sister. I'd love to cuddle a baby and take it for walks in its pram,' Tori sighed.

Paige hadn't considered it like that. Maybe Amy and Tori were right. She'd thought her friends were the lucky ones and now it seemed like they envied her.

Tori suddenly grinned. 'Anyway,' she said, changing the subject. 'I thought this was supposed to be a scary sleepover. I've not exactly been scared of anything yet.'

Paige saw Storm dive under the

bedclothes and then felt a familiar prickling sensation. What was he up to?

'Whoooo! Whoooo!' A loud noise wailed suddenly. All the spiders, bats and ghost shapes leapt off the walls and zoomed towards the end of the bed, where they hovered in the air before shooting back into place.

'Argh!' Tori screamed delightedly. 'That was brilliant. How did you do it?'

'Sound effects and . . . er . . . hidden wires,' Paige said, winking at Storm as he reappeared and snuggled up next to her.

'I nearly wet myself with fright!' Amy exclaimed. 'This is the best party ever.'

'Until mine, next year . . . what?' Tori said as Paige and Amy grabbed a pillow each and battered her.

They made a pact to stay up all night, but after playing Paige's Hunt the Monster game and giggling for an hour as they swapped silly jokes, they snuggled down together. Amy and Tori went to sleep first.

'Goodnight, Storm,' Paige whispered, her eyelids drooping.

'Goodnight, Paige,' Storm woofed, sighing contentedly.

Paige's eyes snapped open. A noise somewhere outside the house had woken her. She reached for Storm, but there was only a tiny warm place next to her where the puppy had been.

Paige crept quietly out of bed, so that she didn't wake Tori and Amy, and tiptoed out on to the dark landing.

From the window, she could see two fierce dogs sniffing about in the front garden. Moonlight glinted on their pale eyes and extra-sharp teeth.

Paige gasped. Shadow's dogs! Storm was in terrible danger. The moment she had been dreading was here. Her heart pounded as she knew she was going to have to be strong for Storm's sake.

Suddenly, a bright flash of gold light streamed out from the open bathroom door at the far end of the landing. Paige threw herself forward and rushed inside.

Storm stood there, a tiny spotty puppy no longer, but a majestic young silver-grey wolf with a glittering neck-ruff. An older she-wolf with a gentle face stood next to him.

Tears pricked Paige's eyes. 'Your enemies are here! Save yourself, Storm!' she burst out.

Storm's big midnight-blue eyes narrowed with affection. 'You have been a true friend, Paige. Be of good heart,' he said in a velvety growl.

'I'll never forget you, Storm,' Paige said, her voice catching.

There was a final dazzling flash and big gold sparks filled the bathroom and floated down around Paige and crackled as they hit the floor. Storm and his mother faded and then were gone.

A furious snarling sounded outside in the front garden, but then all was silent.

Paige stood there, still stunned by how fast it had all happened. Her heart ached, but she was glad that she'd had a chance to say goodbye to her magical friend. She knew that she would always remember the time she'd spent with him.

She looked up with tears in her eyes to see Debs standing there. 'Paige? Did the telephone wake you? Keith's just phoned. You've got a beautiful baby brother. He was born a few minutes ago. Apparently he's got the most amazing dark-blue eyes.'

Just like Storm, Paige thought, with a

sense of wonder. She had a sudden
thought. 'What time is it?' she asked.

'About ten minutes to midnight,'
Debs told her.

Her little brother had been born on
her birthday! She was a big sister now.
Paige felt an unexpected warmth flood
through her at the thought of meeting
her tiny helpless brand-new little
brother. Wherever he was, she knew
that Storm was smiling in approval.

Win a Magic Puppy goody bag!

The evil wolf Shadow has ripped out part of Storm's
letter from his mother and hidden the words so that magic puppy
Storm can't find them.

Storm needs your help!

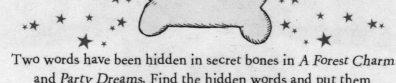

Two words have been hidden in secret bones in *A Forest Charm*
and *Party Dreams*. Find the hidden words and put them
together to complete the message from Storm's mother.
Send it in to us and each month we will put every correct message
in a draw and pick out one lucky winner, who will receive
a Magic Puppy gift – definitely worth barking about!

Send the hidden message, your name and address on a postcard to:
Magic Puppy Competition
Puffin Books
80 Strand
London WC2R 0RL
Good luck!

puffin.co.uk

Coming Soon

Magic Puppy

A little puppy, a sprinkling of magic, a forever friend.

Twirling Tails

School of Mischief

puffin.co.uk

If you like Magic Puppy, you'll love **Magic Kitten**

A Summer Spell
9780141320144

Classroom Chaos
9780141320151

Star Dreams
9780141320168

Double Trouble
9780141320175

Moonlight Mischief
9780141321530

A Circus Wish
9780141321547

Sparkling Steps
9780141321554

A Glittering Gallop
9780141321561

Seaside Mystery
9780141321981

Firelight Friends
9780141321998

A Shimmering Splash
9780141322001

A Puzzle of Paws
9780141322018

A Christmas Surprise
9780141323237

Picture Perfect
9780141323480

A Splash of Forever
9780141323497